L.L.C. *Lust*

Lies and Confessions

LaShae Berry

Archway Publishing books may be ordered through booksellers or by contacting:

Archway Publishing
1663 Liberty Drive
Bloomington, IN 47403
www.archwaypublishing.com
1-(888)-242-5904

ISBN: 978-1-4808-1081-5 (sc)
ISBN: 978-1-4808-1080-8 (e)

Library of Congress Control Number: 2014916984

Printed in the United States of America.

Archway Publishing rev. date: 11/14/2014

The Mission . . .

When a woman knows what she deserves, she is bound to own it. She has a need and a want. A need is different from a want. A woman wants two things: love and protection. She wants to know that a man can love her like he can never love another, and make her feel that love even when he's not around. She wants financial stability: not just "You got my bills, boo," but the financial want that the two are of one accord. A woman wants protection from a man who would shield her with his arms and not back down when it comes to his lady.

The Bible says that when a man finds a wife, he finds a good thing. That is true, but does he really know what it takes to keep that woman? That brings us back to the need of a woman, and that need is desire with fire. She may be getting it three or four times a week, but is he hitting it till she needs it morning, noon, and night?

See, a man can make love to a woman, but she needs to be pleasured. She needs to feel that he is the man that can enter her golden gates, to which he holds the key. Nowadays that's hard to find. Just because she is smiling after his work is done doesn't mean he handled the job or can keep the job. They say she runs for his shoe size, yet the package that he supplies doesn't seem to put out the flames; there's just a quick dash to smother the fire that still burns.

A woman needs feelings from a man, not only the growth of him but his involvement in her. She need to be touched like a runaway slave who was terrified after escaping but is free at last, free at last. She needs to know if he is that man. This may be her only, last, and final seximony, but it was worth the trial to climb and reach her destination on a mission of pleasure. This is how you know you have fulfilled your mission. You approach with a master plan. Never underestimate a woman's worth. She is worth more than all the medals a man can receive in his lifetime. She is the trophy.

Part 1

Chapter 1

Finally the doors were closed, and everyone had left the room except for Carmen and Malcolm. It wasn't a secret that something physical concerning Carmen was going on in the back of Malcolm's head, as she noticed through his suit. She turned her back to him as she placed her wineglass on the counter. She realized she had drunk too many glasses for one night, so she decided to call it quits.

She wanted to get Malcolm's attention but didn't want to make it seem she was desperate for his eye. *Oh yeah, he noticed.* He walked over with a smooth lean that said without words, *I got to get to that.* He approached Carmen and said, "You had fun tonight." She smiled, looking into his eyes, and nodded yes, without any hesitation. Malcolm looked at Carmen and rolled his tongue across his lips from side to side, then gave her a wink. "I'm just going to cut to the chase," he said, "and tell you what I want."

Carmen felt her breathing stop, because she had heard the talk about Malcolm Rhodes and the package that he carried. He was a lover boy, and love is what he gave. That was after his divorce from his wife, who told her girlfriends how her ex-husband put it down, and then one of her girlfriends found out for herself.

Malcolm leaned over and whispered in Carmen's ear, "I want you." Carmen's eyes rolled upward as he softly spoke, sending chills through her body, chills that said, *Like, hell yeah, you can get it, and you can get it all.* She didn't know what to say but started breathing harder. He grabbed her by the waist, pulling her toward him, so she could feel what she could have. It was there, thick, hard, and warm, set and ready for action. “You feel it,” Malcolm said, as he stared down at Carmen.

He grabbed her butt in the palm of his hand and took a big squeeze. He lowered his head and kissed Carmen on the neck, making her moan and say, “Yessss, don’t stop.” Carmen was reaching a level she thought she would never attain, but it took a man with whom she had no relationship to get her there. She was feeling things that Randy had never made her feel. Not even Randy’s touch could make her feel the way she did right then with Malcolm. Not only did Malcolm kiss her on the neck, but his tongue made its way up to her earlobe, giving her a hint of how wet she could really be.

He whispered to her, “Are you getting wet yet?” Carmen started nibbling her bottom lip as she slowly ran her fingers across Malcolm’s chest. He then kissed Carmen on the edge of her jaw, moving toward her lips. Just as he was about to kiss her, the door opened, and Randy yelled at someone to have a good night and a safe drive home. He interrupted what was about to go down—what really could have gone down in a few more moments. Malcolm stopped and walked away quickly, showing no sign that he was doing anything wrong.

Randy walked into the room with no clue that his girl and best friend were getting wet with their clothes on. Or so they thought. Randy knew Malcolm’s postdivorce reputation.. He gave them a stare but shook it off as if to say, *Nah, not here in the open*. Randy walked over to Carmen and held her by the waist. “Well, Malcolm,” said Randy, “you good?”

“Great,” Malcolm replied. Randy thought that the fundraiser would boost business for Malcolm and him. Randy also asked Malcolm whether he had found a new Mrs. Rhodes tonight. The only thing that he had found was giving his best friend and partner's fiancée the time of her life.

"Nah, man," Malcolm said, winking at Carmen when Randy turned his head for just one second. It might be wrong to hit on Carmen, Malcolm thought, but it would feel right whenever he got a chance to hit it just right and make a grown woman want to scream, "Give me the business!"

Carmen knew how bad Malcolm wanted her, and for sure she wanted him. She was in a state of mind that said, *Damn, I want this man bad.* She was getting turned on just by looking at him and the things he did before Randy walked in. She felt her body twerking and getting so overheated that she was beyond ready, about to explode. Carmen knew there was no chance of her getting with Malcolm, so she was ready to give it up to Randy and pretend that he was Malcolm. Carmen cleared her throat and said she wanted to step out onto the patio for some fresh air while Randy and Malcolm talked.

Randy walked toward the bar, asking Malcolm if he wanted another drink before they discussed the fund-raiser that had just gone down and how their business could benefit from it. Randy's back faced Malcolm, who was fixing him a drink, while Malcolm watched every move that Carmen made. Carmen went toward the patio door and looked back. Knowing that Malcolm was watching her, she smiled, looking him over from head to toe. Malcolm stared, while holding his belt loops and then grabbed his package and pointed at Carmen. She walked outside, waving her hand across her face, trying to fan the cool air on her.

"Don't stay out too long, babe," said Randy. "I don't want you to catch a cold."

"Yes, dear," she said, still managing to get a sneak peek at Malcolm.

Time passed quickly; things were wrapping up, and Malcolm was about to leave. Carmen was back in the house after cooling down her hot box. Randy walked Malcolm to the door, seeing him off. Malcolm told Randy and Carmen to have a good night and waved as he was leaving. But it wasn't over yet, because the way he looked at Carmen let her know that he still wanted it.

Chapter 2

The night was just getting started. Randy had no idea that Carmen was feeling the way she was after the time she had spent alone with Malcolm. She knew it was wrong to feel a sexual connection with Malcolm, knowing that her fiancé was a business partner with this man. She loved Randy, but he didn't make her feel the way Malcolm did. She felt a heat inside when she was around him, not the warmth of friendship but the heat of fire in desire.

Yes, she and Randy made love regularly, but he didn't hit it the way she wanted to feel it. Sometimes she lay there and took in what he brought, but it did not satisfy her body. A woman knows what she wants and how she wants it. What a woman wants, she definitely is going to get. Carmen pranced around the room. She couldn't stay still, thinking about Malcolm.

She went to the bathroom before Randy came up and turned on the shower, right up until the steam formed on the mirror, leaving a light, gray haze, blinding the eye. She slipped off the dress she was wearing. She opened the door to the shower, stepped in, and tilted her head back as the flow of the hot water rolled down her body. She lathered up some body wash on a foam ball and began moving it all over her body. Not only was the heat working up tension, but the foam from the body wash was starting to feel good against Carmen's skin. All kinds of thoughts flowed. Nasty, rough thoughts that wanted one man's attention—and it wasn't Randy's.

Flashbacks arose from when she and Malcolm had been alone for just a few minutes, and they wouldn't go away. Carmen began to run her hands across her body as the feel of the soap added more desire. Ooh, her body really started to feel something. She imagined Malcolm's hands all over her. The two of them bare-ass naked in the shower together, getting their freak on. The temperature of the water was just right—hot and steamy—but the more intense Carmen got, the more the heat from the shower turned her on. The lather was feeling so good to her that her thoughts about Malcolm were stuck on wondering how big he really was and whether he put it down. She knew for a fact that he wasn't small, from when he pulled her close to him earlier, giving her the motion of what he was storing.

Not a mind-blowing point came to her about Randy and all he had to offer, just the fact that he didn't make her feel tingly inside. "Damn," she said as she placed her back against the wall, fantasizing about Malcolm, setting the standards high. She fantasized about the way he licked his lips when he talked and the way he moved. His walk was too sexy and smooth; he took his time, with no rush. She figured that was the way he would treat a woman in his arms. How she wished she were in his arms at that moment and, better yet, underneath him. She began to moan.

When Randy finally made it to the bedroom to undress, Carmen opened the door to the bathroom, dripping wet and naked, and said, "I got to have it." Randy was surprised, but excitement and arousal distracted him from wondering what had gotten into Carmen. He was willing to play a role in what Carmen had planned. Carmen walked up close to him, pushing him down on the bed, slowly gliding her body on top of his. She reached her saddle position, leaned forward, and whispered, "I'm ready."

Randy caressed the back of her head and said, "Let me make love to you." Carmen was willing to take Randy to fulfill her thoughts of Malcolm. He started kissing her but not the way she wanted. He began touching her, but she didn't feel the pleasure. He unzipped his pants, and he was standing at attention. But it still wasn't what Carmen wanted. She wanted a man who knew how to take control, and Randy was just about turning her fantasy into a blowout. She rolled over, leaving Randy looking as if he had done something wrong. Enough was enough; if she wanted her fantasy, she had to take it into her own hands. She got back on top, unbuttoned Randy's shirt, kissing him on the neck as she reached down, grabbing him. She kissed Randy as her body rocked back and forth. He got the message, rolled her onto her back, and went to work. He did his usual role play and position, but that didn't bother Carmen. She just closed her eyes and felt Malcolm. In having sex with Randy, she got a real dick to achieve the fantasy she needed.

Carmen moaned and screamed as she never had before. Randy knew he was the man, because he had Carmen calling him Daddy. Foolish! He wasn't even close in Carmen's mind to having that title. She used him and got the satisfaction she needed from her thoughts of another man. Carmen reached her highest climax after twerking her body around as Randy was beating it up. He paused, done now, with a smile on his face, giving that last push in before pulling out. Carmen opened her eyes and stared in the face of her fiancé feeling almost disgusted knowing she used Randy. She realized what she had done, but when a woman wants it, there's no stopping how she will get it.

Chapter 3

After releasing the pressure of desire, Randy was fast asleep, and lonely Carmen was up, wanting a taste of something sweet. She already felt bad thinking about another man while making love to her fiancé, but that didn't stop what she was still feeling. She wanted Malcolm and there was only one way to get him; that was to make her move. She looked at Randy as he slept, knowing that this would hurt him, but curiosity was working on the cat. The way Malcolm moved made her curious. The way he touched her made her weaker. When he kissed her—just thinking about it, her unsatisfied wet box overflowed with lust.

Carmen looked over once more, making sure that Randy was in a deep sleep. She got up from bed and walked over to Randy's side, where his cell phone lay on the nightstand. She grabbed it and hers as well and walked out to the hallway. She went into the bathroom and sat on the floor. She was determined to get what she wanted. She searched through Randy's phone to find Malcolm's number. Once she found it, she began to text him on her phone.

Malcolm, are you up?

She waited for a response on the cold floor, trying to cool off her overheated cootle that was driving her hormones to a raging flame. Minutes later, a text came through.

I'm up, but who is this?

Carmen told him, said that she just wanted to talk to him. That may have been true, but Malcolm knew what the deal was at two in the morning.

I've been waiting, he texted, *wondering how long it was going to take you to get to this moment.*

I can't sleep and my body is weak.

Where is your man?

Asleep in the bedroom.

What do you want from me?

Right now, words to freeze my heat.

Why don't you meet me outside at the gate?

That I can't do. We can't get caught, and besides, I shouldn't have texted.

You only texted because you wanted it, so let me.

Talk to me, Malcolm, and make me feel something.

S*ure, but since I can't come get you, answer the phone. I'm calling.*

The phone lit up, and quickly Carmen answered it. In a sexy, deep voice, Malcolm said, "I want to lick you up and down, starting from your neck, and make you scream to where you're soaking wet. The freak in me can take you places and have your body craving, shivering like a newborn baby. I know how you want it, so I'll pick you up and put my face in it. Are you ready? Tender spots as my tongue roll in it, your legs can't take it. You're jerking like you're having a seizure. Make you feel something, go to work with my key to your trunk. In and out, I got you screaming loud. Hush a moment, and make sure your man is not around. I hear you breathing, moaning and groaning. I wish I was there in your whirlpool, feeling myself swirling inside of you. Yes, yes, I hear you. Are your two fingers wet yet from this excitement, because my volcano is about to erupt, I'm standing straight up. Damn, baby, I'm almost there. Shit, I just came. So did I fuck the hell out of your curiosity?"

Carmen's moaning and groaning woke Randy from his sleep. A knock on the door, his voice asking her was she okay. It scared her to death, and she threw the phone behind the toilet. Randy came in, saw Carmen on the floor, and wondered what was wrong and why it sounded like she was crying. She made up an excuse that her period had started and that she was cramping. He helped her off the floor and asked if she needed anything. She replied no and said she would be there in a minute. Randy kissed Carmen on the forehead and walked away.

Carmen knew she had to get rid of Randy, and to make sure Malcolm didn't hang up. She grabbed the phone from behind the toilet and said "Hello" in a soft tone.

"So you're on your period," said Malcolm.

She whispered, "I almost got caught. This can't happen again."

Shaking and nervous, her curiosity was put on a pause. It didn't stop Malcolm from wanting more. He wanted to meet and give her what her man lacked. "I want you," Malcolm said, "and I'm going to have you." Silence filled the room, except for Carmen's breathing hard into the phone. She said good-bye, said this never happened, but Malcolm knew he had Carmen right where he wanted her. She went to the bedroom and lay down beside Randy. He held her in his arms, but tears formed in Carmen's eyes, as she thought of her wrongdoing.

Chapter 4

Right before Randy left for work, he kissed Carmen on the lips, telling her he loved her, that he was coming home early, and that he would see her in a few hours. Carmen smiled, but she knew that was a lie. Randy catered to that job, and she was on the back burner. She got only whatever time was left over for her.

She showered so that she could go and meet up with a friend to make arrangements with the wedding planner. Randy didn't mind that he wasn't a part of the whole wedding planning; he just wanted Carmen happy, and he was okay with whatever she decided. Money can't bring eternal happiness when a woman feels neglected, but time will tell when she gets fed up.

She dressed and drove to meet Toni, her best friend and maid of honor. They met up at Charlotte's Boutique to talk with the owner about the vision she had for the wedding. Charlotte related her vision of how she was going to make this a spectacular wedding, one Carmen and Randy would never forget. Romance on the beach—what else a woman could ask for than a wedding by the stunning water? As she spoke, Carmen's face lit up, for Charlotte's vision was on point with hers. Except that in her mind she was marrying Malcolm. If only Charlotte could read Carmen's mind!

The ladies drank wine and gathered around, talking about the big day. Toni looked at Carmen and asked, "Are you ready, truly ready?"

"Yes," Carmen said, while visualizing "yes" to the wrong man.

She wanted to be tied down to one man, but the desire for another was interfering. Lust was taking control and wasn't easing up. As the ladies talked, sharing their views about the wedding and marriage, period, all Carmen saw was the nakedness of Malcolm. She could see Malcolm standing before her naked, with a tender sword, ready to charge onto the battlefield. Carmen hormones was rising. Malcolm showed her a side she had been missing out on, and she was ready for a touchdown from a fully equipped quarterback.

"Carmen! Carmen!" yelled Toni. "Are you listening?"

Carmen was in another world, one involving whipped cream and a tall, dark chocolate man. "What?" said Carmen.

Toni and Charlotte looked at each other pointedly; Carmen clearly didn't have her mind on planning her own wedding. That left Toni puzzled about Carmen's future with Randy; her curiosity was getting the best of her. She wondered what was on Carmen's mind. Toni sensed that there was something different about Carmen. Carmen laughed it off as she screamed, "Yes, I'm ready!"

She didn't want to make it obvious that she had concerns about marrying Randy, not even letting it slip that she had a connection with Malcolm. Carmen felt she was wasting her time and energy on a man who was settled in his ways, that a change was never going to happen. Randy wanted a family, but bringing a baby into the picture right now would lead to disaster. A woman might show happiness on the outside, acting like everything was great, yet destruction was tearing her down on the inside. Randy never took the time to get to know Carmen emotionally, which led her to say, "I'd rather be alone for the rest of my life than to be sad and miserable in a trap." These are the feelings of an unclosed wound drowning in a river of hurt and pain.

Chapter 5

Carmen was on her way home after meeting with Charlotte when she looked down and saw she had received a text message. She opened it, and damn, it was Malcolm. He had sent her a picture of him with an attached message: *This is what you're missing.* Carmen almost ran off the side of the road, stunned by what she saw. Malcolm sent her a picture of him in his birthday suit, with nothing on but his cowboy boots and a hat, and holding his penis in his hand.

Heat started rising up Carmen's body, putting her into such a sweat that she had to roll down the window. "Damn, what a big dick," she said. Before she could say anything else, the phone rang. She answered it, not knowing who it was, because the number showed as restricted.

It was Malcolm. In a sexy whisper, he said, "I want you, meet me. Carmen braked in the middle of the road, taking a deep breath. Luckily, there was no one behind her when she slammed on her brakes. She knew that Malcolm and Randy was together at the moment, but that didn't stop Malcolm from calling his best friend's fiancée. Malcolm wanted to meet Carmen at a hotel on the other side of town from where Randy would be handling business. Carmen wanted to say no, but focusing on the picture she received made her more anxious to say yes.

"Randy will be inside for a while for a meeting," said Malcolm, "but I need to go and do an errand." Carmen's mouth dropped open.

After clearing her throat, she said, "Yes, I'll meet you." It was on and about to start popping.

They both hung up, and off she drove, convinced that she was getting her some; surely her body was ready for some. Just seconds away from meeting Malcolm, something unexpected was about to happen. After arriving at the hotel, as she got out she noticed a man waving at her. She looked puzzled as he approached. It was Jonathan, one of Randy's golf buddies. He was leaving the hotel after a meeting with the president of the golf tournament that would be taking place next weekend. She was caught by surprise when he asked her what she was up to and how the wedding planning was going. Carmen made up an excuse that she was there to pick up a friend who was in from out of town helping her with the wedding.

A close call. Her phone rang and Malcolm walked out the front door to see why it was taking Carmen so long. She was hoping that Jonathan would leave. She knew then that it was over, and she had to let Malcolm know that it wasn't going to happen. Malcolm looked up and ducked back in after seeing Carmen talking to Jonathan. The phone stopped ringing, and a text came through. Jonathan noticed that Carmen looked anxious, so he said good-bye and moved on. Malcolm texted Carmen to see what was up. She texted back, *Good-bye.*

Carmen walked back to her car, shaking with fear. Jonathan drove off waving and disappeared. Malcolm approached the right side of Carmen's car. "Damn, baby, let me explore," he said. Carmen was too scared to make another move. She was afraid everything would get back to Randy. Malcolm walked over to Carmen's side, brushing up against her. Her knees became weak, and she almost went down to the ground. Malcolm was still ready for action; it didn't bother him a bit that they almost got caught.

"It's too risky," Carmen said. She said they should go their own separate ways for the time being. An experience was about to happen, but too much was rising up to shut the game down. Even though one door closes, another one surely leaves a crack. At least Plan B was on Malcolm's agenda.

Part 2

Chapter 6

Carmen was trying to convince herself that she was still in love with Randy and wasn't done with love, even though her feelings kept her wondering about Malcolm and the package that he was carrying. She felt like her glass was empty, and a refill would be the perfect fix. It had been a long time for Carmen to be held by a man the way she wanted to be held. Hell, any man really. She wanted more than what Randy was giving her. The sex had slowed down, and so did the attention that she had been getting at the start of their relationship. Randy was so much on a mission to get this big-time corporation to sign with his company that he forgot that he was in a relationship. It was on thin ice, according to Carmen; she was on a mission herself, and it wasn't getting attention anymore from her own man, but from one man: Malcolm. Randy spent most of his time on the golf course with his client, trying to warm up a deal, then Malcolm went in for the kill. But the way to celebrate, after all is said and done, he would send Malcolm to deliver gifts to Carmen to make her a part of it, showing his love. If only he knew the love wasn't given back for him. That didn't bother Malcolm, besides he had a plan of his own. Just unexpected, Carmen was thinking Randy didn't forget that the two of them had a lunch date, that she was dressed for not leaving the house, in black see-through baby-doll lingerie with red six-inch high heels. What was on the menu? Not food. The door bell rang, and Carmen had every intention that it was Randy who was about to get a surprise. She opened the door with her head tilted back, hair down, saying in a sexy tone, "What took you so long?"

"Damn," said Malcolm, "I'm here."

Carmen was the one surprised. She was in an awkward position but really didn't mind what happened. It didn't stop Malcolm from the jump, because he grabbed Carmen by the waist and started kissing her. He moved in closer, closing the door behind him. She knew it was all over with; it was going down. *Fiancé who*? Carmen felt the rush and didn't want to come down until it was over. Malcolm had his way finally, and he wasn't letting up. He turned Carmen around, her back to him, and ran his hand up her thigh, pulling down her lacy thong. Carmen moaned and groaned, saying "Yes, don't stop." That was fine with Malcolm; stopping wasn't on his mind.

She stood against the wall as he got down on his knees with her legs spread. He put his tongue on her as he licked down her thighs. He removed her thong from around her ankles and lay on his back and asked her to bend down. She got down on her knees, covering his face, and he went to work. Carmen closed her eyes and experienced the magic of oral sex for the first time by someone who knew about the fruit bowl. Malcolm's tongue moved around while his lips rested on the outside of Carmen's vagina.

Carmen's body began to move around. He picked her up by her thighs and started raising her up and down against his tongue. You'd think his tongue lifted weights, because each time she came down, he was pointed in the right direction and never missed. Carmen's legs starting shaking, and the screams got louder and louder. Carmen was screaming, "Yes, Malcolm! Yes, oh Daddy!" and that drove Malcolm crazy. He wanted it and wanted it right now. He raised Carmen up, setting her on her feet; then he stood and started to unzip his pants. At the same time the phone was ringing. That didn't stop the two of them from getting a hit off of each other. The phone stopped ringing and went to the answering machine. Malcolm was right at the edge of entering, with Carmen bent over, touching the floor. The message came through; it was Toni, who was ten minutes away.

"Damn," said Malcolm as he rushed to put on his clothes and dip before Toni arrived. Carmen walked Malcolm to the door, looking disappointed, but Malcolm knew something that Carmen didn't. So he kissed her on the neck and rushed off without mentioning a word to Carmen about what he had up his sleeve. Carmen closed the door, weak in her knees, not because of Toni but from still feeling the explosion from Malcolm's tongue.

Forgotten all about the gift, Malcolm rushed back, he rang the doorbell but before he said, "Baby, open up," Toni startled him from behind. Toni gave him a look like, *What the hell are you doing here*? Malcolm handed Toni the gift, stating he was to deliver it to Carmen from Randy. Toni noticed Malcolm's pants were unzipped. Carmen opened the door, looking stunned that Malcolm was still here and with Toni. Carmen stuttered as she tried to speak. Toni handed Carmen the gift and walked in, leaving Malcolm to rush to his car. Toni turned to Carmen and said, "Explain." It didn't take a genius to know something had gone down.

Chapter 7

Nine o'clock, and Randy decided to come home from playing golf. It wasn't enough to fill the broken heart of a woman who was fed up with an unappreciative man, even though Randy came home with extra gifts, a bouquet of flowers, and a box of "I'm sorry" chocolate. Silence filled the room as Carmen walked away from Randy. She went into the bedroom and slammed the door behind her, locking it, and stuffed her head into the pillow. Tonight she cried tears over an unwanted man, but tonight would be the last night; her pool was drained dry. Love was put to a test. Love is like water, without the right current, the flow of the boat won't sail, but a rescue ship is never too far away. The cork in the hole in Randy's boat was loose, and he didn't have a life jacket aboard. Randy tried to sweet-talk Carmen, but she wasn't hearing a sound from an ungrateful son of a bitch who forgot that he was engaged, or even that he had a woman at home who would let him fuck her brains out.

Instead, his best friend was two inches away from getting the job done. Carmen felt abused by a workaholic man. She was mistreated by lack of attention from a self-centered figure. She felt choked, gasping for air, but this ass of a man failed to rescue her. Only months away from their wedding day, and the thought rose in her head that *she* objected.

Randy let her blow off steam, to have her way and be mad. But all she wanted was for him to be a man and grab her and shake her, then lay the law down and make her scream, to act like he wanted her and nothing else. *Is that too much to ask for from a man you are about to submit to?* she thought. She knew there were two sides to a story, so what was Randy really hiding?

Randy didn't get as much as a kiss good-night, but a cold, lonely room that he slept in alone. The guest bedroom was all the action he was getting. At that moment he felt like a guest in his own home. Even though he let Carmen be, Randy had no clue why she stayed so mad at him. He knew he was a good man who provided and gave Carmen anything and everything. He took care of Carmen and the bills, but he didn't see that the one thing he lacked as a man, which put their relationship in jeopardy, was feelings. What a man can't see to fix, another man finds and gets on the job.

Chapter 8

Five days later Randy still didn't get the picture. The two were supposed to meet up and discuss with the wedding planner the finishing touches to the wedding, and once again he stood Carmen up. She and Charlotte went over her vision of the rehearsal. Carmen's mind wasn't fixed on hearing about the wedding less long putting her input on it. Carmen had come to a realization, and she knew she had to deal with it. She was falling in love with Malcolm and falling out of love with Randy. The flashbacks of her and Malcolm the day they almost got caught rose to the surface. She started thinking nasty thoughts with her eyes closed; her head rolled back. Not even concerned that she was in a public place, she imagined Malcolm's hands all over her, from head toe. Charlotte kept calling Carmen's name until she came back to reality.

"What are you doing?" asked Charlotte.

Carmen was momentarily speechless but quickly spoke up. "I was trying to visualize the setting," she said, trying to throw Charlotte off.

Yes, she was visualizing, but not some*thing*. It was some*one,* who had a peekaboo surprise for a box, with the right key to fit it. Carmen received a text from Toni stating her whereabouts and wanting to know if Carmen was free for a minute. Toni knew that Carmen's day was busy, but she thought it was busy with Randy.

Charlotte had to show Carmen something about the wedding that made her forget to respond to Toni's message. Charlotte wasn't curious about why Randy wasn't there; he hadn't shown up even one time for the planning of the wedding. But a tall chocolate man opened the door, and Carmen's jaw dropped. Malcolm stepped in and all eyes were on him. Charlotte asked if she could help him, but he knew exactly what he was there for. Carmen's face glowed like a disco ball on a Friday night. Her tongue slid inside her mouth while she stroked Malcolm from head to toe with her eyes. Malcolm was there to deliver Carmen a check for the balance for the wedding expenses.

Tell me, what man sends his best friend on an errand with his wife-to-be? thought Carmen. *If only Randy knew the thoughts that are rolling around in our heads, he would keep a close eye on us.*

Things started heating up, especially after Carmen wanted Malcolm to stay and fill in for Randy. Charlotte gave Carmen a look. Charlotte had an idea that something was going on but stayed out of it; she had her money. No one knows what a woman goes through in a relationship until all hell breaks loose.

After Malcolm stayed and everyone felt each other's vibe, the planning proceeded, with secret lust and smiles and laughter. *What's done in the mind won't hurt anybody*, Carmen thought, but she was about to explode. Charlotte left the room for just a second, leaving Carmen and Malcolm unattended. He talked to Carmen about a deal that Randy and he were working on that would take them out of town for about two days, but he felt that he was going to be sick and couldn't make it. "If you know what I mean," he said. Malcolm had a plan, a romance plan that could finally make his and Carmen's fantasy become reality.

Malcolm spoke in a sexy tone, but swiftly. "I want you those two days and want to make you scream until you tell me you've had enough." Carmen took deep breaths as her finger left her lips, and she crossed her legs from her excitement at seeing the bulge in Malcolm's pants. "Let me hit it right," said Malcolm, "and you won't worry about crossing your legs."

Carmen was on fire. She could have stripped down to her G-string and given it up on Charlotte's table. Damn, this man was giving her the business. The sound of Charlotte's heels approached, but before she walked in, Carmen asked Malcolm when and where. *Randy who? So long, boo.*

Carmen was on her way to getting fixed. Her motor needed to be blown out, and it had been a pain finding the right mechanic. Carmen wanted a jerk then and there, a full speed of lust rushing to her brain, then spreading all over her like she was standing under a waterfall. Malcolm packed the speed and the force she desired.

Charlotte watched the two but made no sudden move. Without any acknowledgment that they weren't alone, the passion showed strongly between the two. Charlotte and Carmen were done for the day. Malcolm walked toward the door, looked back, and held it open for Carmen, but Charlotte stopped Carmen to have a word with her in private. Charlotte asked Carmen if she was ready for marriage. Carmen looked puzzled and said "Yes, why?" Charlotte shook her head and responded with "To who?" That was the last word. Carmen left with the expression telling Charlotte to bug off and mind her own business. Love hurts sometimes, but lust can be a temporary fix.

Chapter 9

Love does hurt sometimes, and lust has that magic touch to put a patch over the open wounds just enough to cover the pain. Malcolm was hurting, hurting with desire, wanting this woman so deeply that he didn't care who knew. As he was escorting Carmen to her car, he watched her from behind. She had a swish in her walk, shaking what her mama gave her. Those thick thighs blew him away as he viewed the fitted dress she wore lead him on a different path. Those same thighs tied around his waist—yet another thought wrapped around his neck. The more she walked, the harder he got; whenever she spoke, the more he wanted to poke. The mood was fast and frisky.

It was only moments from leaving the wedding planner that Carmen had almost the exact feelings. She knew Malcolm was watching her, so she threw it as hard as she could to keep his attention. Finally she made it to her car, so she "accidentally" dropped her keys, so that she would bend down and touch her toes. She really wanted to make sure Malcolm had a full view. View or not, Malcolm was on it. As Carmen bent down, Malcolm grabbed her by her waist. "Do you feel that?" he said. Carmen moaned yes. Malcolm was relaxed, but something else was getting stiff. Malcolm waved like the motion of the ocean as he squeezed Carmen closer, almost lifting her feet off the ground. He for damn sure knew what he wanted and Carmen was willing to give. Suddenly Carmen's phone started ringing, but that didn't stop the two. Then a text came through. What the hell, that wasn't an alarm either.

Carmen had what she wanted with her. She closed her eyes as she slowly raised up her dress, giving Malcolm a surprise glance of the lace of her panties. Malcolm didn't deny the invitation, so he helped lift her dress up until it reached the lower part of her back, then slowly pulled down her lacy panties to her knees. Carmen spread her legs wider, since the two of them were in an area in the parking lot where they couldn't be seen. Malcolm used one hand to feel himself, then gently slid the zipper of his pants down. Peekaboo. He was ready to aim and fire. Malcolm moved himself back and forth, hitting the crack of Carmen's butt. Each bump made Carmen crave more and more. Bump after bump: once, twice, and the third time spreading the cheeks of Carmen's butt open. Right before she assumed the position, Carmen's phone rang again, this time with a message, but it was still not enough to take her attention away from what was happening. Malcolm and Carmen were too heated, and the race they started was about to get finished.

That is, until a man's voice was heard behind them. Carmen grabbed the side of her mirror trying to raise herself up while pulling down her dress. She kicked off her panties, pushing them underneath the car. Malcolm turned his back toward the gentleman, pretending that he was just talking to Carmen, while rushing to get his pants zipped. The man walked up just three cars away, saying hello to the two of them, then going on his merry way. Malcolm reached down and picked up Carmen's panties, claiming his treasure, a prize of what he'd almost had. Carmen and Malcolm were in the clear once again. That was what they figured, anyway, until a car happened to pass by as Carmen was kissing Malcolm good-bye, on the lips. It was Toni. She saw what she couldn't believe. Questions rolled in her head, and she was bound to get answers.

Chapter 10

Carmen arrived home with the smell of lust on her, her imagination full of pleasure. She opened the door, and there sat Randy on the couch, reading a magazine. She walked toward the kitchen to get a bottle of cold water out of the refrigerator. She was surprised that Randy was home. He looked at her with a puzzled expression as she walked past him without a word. He quickly grabbed her by the arm, pulling her toward him. Carmen fell into Randy's lap as he politely whispered in her ear, "I'm sorry I wasn't there today. Do you forgive me?"

She looked into his eyes and said, "Yes, dear. I know you are a busy man, but it all worked out." Randy asked Carmen if Malcolm delivered the check to her. "He did, and right on time," she said. This should have alerted Randy that something wasn't right if he paid attention to his fiancé closely, but if a man isn't taking care of his woman or making her feel like a woman, much less giving her pleasure like she is the only woman, he won't catch a thing.

Randy went for a kiss but was rejected. He knew she was mad, and yet the news he was about to tell her wouldn't make it better. Carmen lifted herself, saying, "I'm tired and going to relax." She went to the bedroom, where she undressed for a shower. She turned the water on, getting it just right, hot and steamy. She had her back toward the glass entrance when, caught off guard, she turned around and saw that Randy stood behind her naked, ready for action. She gave him a look as if to say, *Man, please, that doesn't even interest me.* The only package she wanted was attached to another gorgeous chocolate man.

Randy stood with his head down, looking like a sad puppy, thinking Carmen was going to feel sorry for him, forgive and forget, then give him some. He grabbed Carmen by her thighs, lifting her up, spreading her legs, placing her back against the wall of the shower, letting the flow of the water roll down on top of them, hitting the right places to keep the rhythm. He wanted Carmen nice and wet, easy for him to go in. As he held her in his arms, he ran his tongue across her body, kissing every inch that he could. Randy moaned and groaned, telling Carmen how bad he missed her today.

Randy pushed his way in, having that feeling in the back of his head that he was the man and was hitting the corners. Story be told, she would rather be alone and get the right pleasure than be stuck in a relationship getting the wrong pleasure. Carmen and Randy's romance was taking a toll on the way she felt about him. She was beginning to prefer being alone to being with Randy, feeling miserable and sad in their relationship.

As Randy was doing his business, Carmen just wished he would stop. Every sound from him, his moaning "Yes, yes" annoyed her, and the feel of his dick disgusted her. After all was said and done, and Randy had released his pressure, Carmen couldn't wait to wash his scent off her. She showered and rushed out, getting dressed before Randy had any other thing on his mind. Randy walked out naked, smiled at Carmen, and jumped into bed just as he was. Randy started telling her of the deal he had made, and that he and Malcolm would be going out of town for a couple of days. Clearly that was Randy's plan, but Malcolm and Carmen had theirs. It didn't bother her that he was going to be leaving. He never took the time that he did have to spend with her. But this time was different, and while Randy was talking, her thoughts were strictly on Malcolm Rhodes.

Part 3

Chapter 11

Chasing the cat was the mission of the day. That was all that was on Malcolm's mind. The deal went through, and the tickets were set for the next morning's flight. Now it was time to set the trap.

In the meantime, Randy was on trial about how to make it up to Carmen for not meeting with her and Charlotte for putting the last touches to their wedding. At least that is what he thought. It never made sense to Carmen that her man would send another man to do his job, which led her to wonder whether she should marry him and ask for forgiveness or spread her legs and let it happen with Malcolm, although all feelings were leading toward lust. Randy wasn't giving Carmen what she needed. Carmen wanted to feel like a woman, to feel wanted by a man, and, for sure, he had to know what to do with it once he got it.

Randy sent roses to Carmen to make up for his lack of attention to her. That didn't win the case. Not even close. All the flowers and gifts in the world wouldn't make Carmen forgive or forget. Marriage is a big step, and Randy was just taking baby steps in their relationship. He hadn't proven worthy to be her man.

At the office packing what he needed for the trip, Randy was convinced that he was coming back home with a closed deal with the help of his partner. Then he could work on him and Carmen. Malcolm drove up at the office with the perfect excuse. He walked in and shook Randy's hand, smiling with excitement, all riled up about the trip and that they were going to close the deal. Truth be told, Malcolm was excited about the text message he had received from Carmen earlier. Randy went over a few things with Malcolm to clarify how things would go in New York.

Malcolm listened but his mission was Carmen. He texted her, saying, *Let's meet tomorrow morning*. Silly as it was to be having conversations with another man's woman while in the same room with him, Malcolm had to go through with his plan. It was set, the plot and the lovemaking for a yearning woman and a determined man. Tomorrow, sealed, stoled and soon to be wrecked. Meanwhile, back at the condo, Carmen had Randy's luggage packed and ready, just as he wanted it. Randy was a punctual man, never late for anything. But there's a first time for everything, including not being on time for something.

Chapter 12

It was only a matter of time before Carmen was going to explode on her so-called best friend. Carmen received message after message from Toni asking her if she was having an affair with Malcolm. Carmen was in the midst of dropping Randy off at the airport when she received a call from Toni but didn't answer it. As Randy was getting his ticket, Carmen responded to Toni. Carmen replied no to cheating, and that she and Malcolm had nothing going. Toni spilled the beans that she saw the two kissing in the parking lot. The smoke hit the fan, so Carmen had to make up an excuse to get Toni off her back. But Toni wasn't buying it. She felt that Carmen was attracted to Malcolm, so why stop the cat from wanting to try a bone.

"Carmen," Toni said. Without feeling, Carmen listened to what Toni had to say and gently hung up the phone, turning it to silent so that she wouldn't have to explain anything to Toni.

Randy was getting worried about Malcolm. He blew up Malcolm's phone trying to reach him, but no luck. Only fifteen minutes to boarding, and Randy was getting nervous. Carmen rubbed Randy's back, asking him what was wrong, as if she didn't know. Just then Randy's cell phone rang; it was Malcolm calling. "Where are you, man?" demanded Randy.

Malcolm explained frantically that he had tried calling Randy first thing this morning, to let him know that his house had been broken into last night while he wasn't there, and that the cops were there making a report. He couldn't leave. Stupid as the story was, Randy bought it. He told Malcolm to handle his business and that he would take care of New York.

Carmen was thrilled but expressed her concern about Malcolm's home being invaded. The trap was set, the fish bit the bait, and off in the air Randy went. Carmen put on her shades and twirled around in her long, seductive dress, with the attitude *I'm a bad bitch*. She jumped into Randy's Benz, not even watching the plane take off, knowing she was about to be someone else's bitch. Not a care in the world was going to stop her, because Malcolm Rhodes was going to play her bitch.

Chapter 13

A black town car drove up at Carmen and Randy's condo. A very handsome man approached the door, ready to drive Carmen to Hotel Rodgewell, one of the most expensive hotels in the city. "Ms. Carmen Links," said the driver, "your carriage awaits." Carmen pointed out to the driver that he didn't put her bags in the car. He nodded and said that Mr. Rhodes had everything covered and that she was to only bring herself. Malcolm went all out just to spend two days with his partner's fiancée. Carmen stepped into car, and there on the seat lay a bouquet of roses, a tray filled with ice, and one champagne glass with a note attached saying, *Enjoy, because the fun is just getting started.*

Carmen smiled with a giggle as the driver closed the door and drove off. As the driver approached the hotel, Carmen received a call. It was Toni, who wasn't giving up on her lead of Malcolm and Carmen's affair. Carmen let her voice mail catch the message, then turned her phone off. Finally, the romance was about to begin. The hotel doorman had a message to deliver to Carmen: *Dessert first, dinner last.* It didn't take much to know that two plus two equals four play, and Malcolm had all the tricks to make it happen.

He noted, *I'm in room 18,* short for *sexting*, and a smiley face. Carmen rode the elevator to the second floor, where she stood at room 18. She knocked on the door, removing her shades, and there stood that chocolate fine-ass Malcolm, showing his six-pack, smooth chest, and muscular arms, and down below a package that looked as if it was ready to be opened, wearing only some lounge pants that showed he had nothing on underneath them. Carmen, completely breathless, took in what stood before her.

"How are you today?" asked Malcolm, as he thanked Carmen for turning off Randy's phone the night prior. Carmen smacked Malcolm with a kiss to say, "You're welcome."

It didn't take much to get the party started. One to three glasses, yet the passion was already there. One kiss led to another. Before Carmen knew it, Malcolm was sliding her zipper down and removing her dress. Carmen stood nearly naked, but Malcolm was a gentleman and had for her something comfortable and luscious to wear also. Malcolm asked Carmen to remove her panties, for there was no need for them, and to slip on the gown he had bought for her. No turning back now or any interruptions to keep the two from filling each other's needs. Malcolm wrapped his arms around Carmen, pulling her close to him. They kissed and Carmen felt Malcolm's tongue swirling around in her mouth. Malcolm picked Carmen up, placing her on the bed, kissing all over her body. Passion heated up quickly between the two, making the headboard rattle against the wall.

"How bad do you want me?" whispered Malcolm. Carmen spread her legs, showing how bad she wanted him, allowing Malcolm to do as he pleased. Malcolm caressed Carmen's breasts with one hand as he glided down her body with his tongue and lips to her thighs. She screamed, louder and louder until whoever was in the next room knew Malcolm's name. Carmen's body shook with ecstasy. "You're wet," he whispered as he moved forward, positioning himself inside of her. Malcolm picked Carmen up as he was still inside her, giving her the bounce of her life. He then laid her flat and rolled her to her knees, asking, "How rough do you want it?"

Carmen yelled, "Beat it up!"

Whatever pace Malcolm was hitting it, Carmen was screaming for it faster and faster. Malcolm was in the groove, and as it got good to him, the bed banged harder and harder against the wall. Carmen gave in. Carmen's head dropped down as Malcolm pushed and pushed until pressure was released. Carmen got what she wanted: freedom. She was free of her own pressure of desire. She moved around like a waterless fish, still feeling Malcolm inside of her. She looked into his eyes, not even thinking of Randy or his feelings, but knowing it took a real man to handle the job. Malcolm kissed Carmen, sucking her bottom lip. "What about a cigarette now, especially after some amazing sex?"

Malcolm had called for room service to arrive at a certain time. It did, right on time, but the taste of food was the last thing on Malcolm's and Carmen's minds. The food was delivered but also with a warning that complaints had been made about the screaming. The playground wasn't closed yet. Just a nice bath to relax in together, and then the festivity was back on. There was more love Malcolm had to share. More of everything with Malcolm Rhodes.

Chapter 14

Ten forty-five, and Carmen was fast asleep. A night filled with passion every two to three hours, and now the morning began with lust still in the air. It was the second day of burning flames, and Carmen was awakened with strawberries and chocolate for breakfast, with a glass of white wine. Malcolm crawled his way up from the foot of the bed to Carmen, placing his body on top of hers, kissing her on the lips, saying that he didn't want the day to end.

"Has your fiancé called?" Malcolm asked. Carmen jumped up, realizing that she had turned her phone off the day she arrived at the hotel and forgot to turn it back on. What a night of good sex can do to a woman's memory or to her dedication to her relationship! Carmen turned on her phone and saw that she had twelve missed calls from Randy. She pushed the send button, trying to get Randy on the phone. He answered in a sour tone.

"Baby, how are things?" asked Carmen, trying to sweet-talk Randy's tone into turning around.

"Where the hell you been?" Randy yelled.

Once again Carmen covered her butt, telling Randy why her phone was going straight to voice mail. She told Randy she had misplaced her phone and was just now finding it. While Carmen was spilling her heart out to Randy on the phone, Malcolm was making a standing ovation. Carmen tried to rein in her heavy breathing until Randy mentioned that he closed the deal and that he was on his way home in about an hour.

"Okay, baby," said Carmen as she rushed off the phone. That didn't give her and Malcolm more time to spend, so they both packed up and called it quits. For the hotel part, that is. Malcolm wanted to bring down the house. What is a dirty man if he doesn't make his point? He gets the goods from the woman, but how can he finish killing another man's spirit?

The two arrived at the condo, where Malcolm dropped off Carmen. He played the gentleman by walking her to the door, but as a freaky man, he wasn't finished. Malcolm kissed Carmen, and she tried to push him away, knowing that Randy would be home and that she didn't want to get caught. "Stop," she said.

"Why?" asked Malcolm.

"Randy will be home soon."

That didn't stop Malcolm. Instead he said, "Let's get over with morning-after sex."

Carmen looked at the table where there was a picture of her and Randy. She held her head down. She knew she still wanted it, so Carmen faced the picture down on the table and let Malcolm have his way. At his house, in his bed. It didn't matter to Malcolm that the picture of Randy and Carmen stood on the table. Malcolm lay down in Randy's bed with Carmen and went all in for the kill, making sweet love once more with Randy's fiancée. Malcolm knew this was his last chance with Carmen and had a feeling something was bound to happen. Best friends come a dime a dozen, but good sex from a well-known cat crawler was worth seeking.

Chapter 15

Carmen led Malcolm to the front door. Their lips seemed inseparable. Malcolm opened the door with both hands on Carmen's butt, his lips to hers. He didn't want to release yet forcing his hands up her dress showing the thickness of Carmen to whomever. As Carmen's butt showed to the world, she pushed Malcolm away. Malcolm walked away, still with desire in his eyes and the risk in his heart, knowing he played foul.

Moments after Malcolm left, a town car drove up, dropping off Randy. Carmen was about to head for a shower to wash the taste of Malcolm off until the front door opened and Randy walked in. Nervous as she could be, she played it well. Randy smiled as he approached Carmen, placing his lips to hers. Carmen never made it to the shower, so she still had the smell of Malcolm on her body, and yet Randy wasn't backing down. Carmen stopped him and asked, "Have you talked with Malcolm? Her luck was going to come to an end. What you do in the dark will come to light. Randy eventually called Malcolm to make sure that everything went okay with his situation. He asked Malcolm about having dinner, to give him the scoop on how he closed the deal. Malcolm agreed and asked what time and location.

"Seven o'clock at Hotel Rodgewell," answered Randy.

Silence. Malcolm was stunned that Randy picked Hotel Rodgewell. He then declined frantically, saying that he had something to do and that they would catch up later. It wasn't a split second later that the doorbell rang.

Not one to leave well enough alone, Toni was determined to get on the bottom of everything, so she paid Carmen a visit. She had seen the two out kissing in front of the condo. Toni looked at Carmen and said, "What are you doing?"

Carmen once again didn't deny it but didn't confirm it either. "What are you talking about?" she replied.

Toni spoke loud and clear. "You're having a fucking affair with Malcolm."

Carmen couldn't resist telling Toni to mind her own business and to lower her voice because Randy was home. Before Toni could say another word, Randy walked up to the door. Carmen looked at Toni, saying the discussion was closed and that Toni knew her way out. Carmen closed the door, leaving Toni stunned by her remarks. She walked away feeling that her best friend was making a big mistake and that she would lose her husband-to-be. Would Carmen admit to having an affair?

Part 4

Chapter 16

Suspicion weighed on Randy that something was up with Carmen. He had noticed for weeks the cold shoulder, the unexpected messages that Carmen received that led her to leave a room. Randy felt the push away from his fiancée, so for once he tried to be a man and stand for his. Randy made reservations at the hottest spots to get back on board with Carmen, but things would miraculously come up and she couldn't attend. He planned a romantic night that led to watching the stars, but Carmen was nowhere to be found. Randy would text Carmen throughout the day, saying *I love you*, but there was no response from his future wife. After sending flowers upon flowers, lovemaking came to a halt, and their relationship seemed dead.

Doubt finally sank in, and he knew a change had come. Their home didn't feel the same anymore. Whereas Carmen always nearby for him to reach, she began to disappear for long periods of time. Carmen's mood changed and she started to ignore Randy. He tried his best to make it work, but his best just wasn't good enough. This was a woman who was falling out of love with a man who never took time out for her. Randy gave others unneeded attention but practically sent his fiancée into the arms of another man. What Randy didn't know was the closure she got from this man that he never gave out.

Carmen felt like a woman with Malcolm, a woman who was needed as more than a trophy wife. Carmen found her flow of enjoyment, and that was top, bottom, side to side, in front of, or anywhere that she received it from Malcolm. Carmen was in her own world and getting the ride of her life.

Randy knew there was something going on, but cheating was the last thing on his mind. That is, until he received an anonymous text saying, *Don't be fooled by a pretty smile, because that same smile can tell a lie and keep a secre*t. Randy didn't know how to respond to the text. But day after day he would receive a different one. Each had bits of information, each one more step leading to Carmen's bed of lust. Randy received one text too many, which led to him getting his number changed. For weeks he received no messages. He thought that someone had been playing a prank or just had the wrong number. One night after he came home from a meeting, the texting started again. He hit the received button; it said, *Where is your fiancée*? Surprised, he sat down, not knowing how to respond. As he was wondering who this could be, another text hit: *She's with him now.* Enough of this foolishness, the reason why his number had to be changed; he tried to block in his mind that it wasn't about Carmen. Before he could respond, *Who is this?* he received another text stating, *Can your house be the only thing that gets broken into?* Then it started raining messages, until one in particular hit home: *Can you trust roads and where they lead?* His thoughts went to one thing: Malcolm. Malcolm Rhodes.

Chapter 17

Days, then weeks, went by, and Randy played it by ear, noticing every move Carmen made. Not only that, he kept a tight eye on Malcolm. He feared for the future of their marriage. He took matters into his own hands and hired a private investigator, hoping his insecurities would be proven wrong. For a while the messaging stopped, until two days before the wedding rehearsal. Not only did Randy have his own investigation going on, but someone else had theirs and made a shocking move.

Randy received a package at his office. He opened it and found a note: *Believe not what you hear; actions tell all.* With it were pictures of a man and woman in a parking lot about to get intimate, but he couldn't make out the faces. He called the private investigator and asked him questions, but he had no answers about the package Randy received. Meanwhile, he called Carmen, asking her to meet him for lunch, but Carmen made it clear that she had some last-minute errands to do before tomorrow night. Malcolm walked into the office, telling Randy that he was headed out himself for lunch. Randy said okay and asked if he could join him. Malcolm quickly gave Randy an excuse that he had business to take care of and rushed out of the office just as Randy was receiving a call from Jake, the investigator, who stated that he found nothing. Malcolm and Carmen stopped sneaking around after Toni's outburst.

One thing leads to another. Randy took in what Jake told him, but something else sparked, so Randy jumped on it. He followed Malcolm from a distance for thirty minutes away from the office. He saw Malcolm pull into a deserted parking lot of an old, abandoned building. Randy wondered what Malcolm was doing there. Was he involved in something illegal? Randy watched as Malcolm got out of his car and walked into the building, looking behind himself, making sure he wasn't being followed. As Malcolm closed the door, Randy jumped out of his car to take a look for himself, a courageous move, but the outcome was going to be a shocker. Randy peeked in a window and saw Malcolm with his pants down to his knees, moaning and groaning, asking a woman, "Who's your daddy?" He watched intensely, waiting for the female to turn around. After all the banging was done, he got a glimpse of her face. Surely it wasn't Carmen. Randy was relieved to know that it wasn't his fiancée, so he got off Malcolm's trail.

Chapter 18

The night before the wedding rehearsal, Carmen stayed in the bathroom, throwing up. She told Randy it was a twenty-four-hour bug and that it had to run its course. Thing was, she had a feeling that she could be pregnant, and that the baby wouldn't be Randy's.

Randy figured it was the pre-marriage jitters. Carmen climbed into bed, and so did Randy. He covered Carmen with his arms, shielding her the way she always wanted to be held by him, making her feel secure and safe. From her point of view, a baby by the wrong man could cost her to lose everything. She realized now that she had made a big mistake. She experienced a night and a day of burning fire, a few messages, a couple of meet-and-greets here and there. Well, Malcolm got what he wanted and then moved on. Therefore, Carmen and Malcolm cut all lost together.

Still, Malcolm looked Randy in the eye each day, knowing he had been in between Carmen's legs. As Carmen and Randy lay in bed, a feeling suddenly rose over her. A spark hit her as Randy lay there beside her, rubbing his hands on her body. It was a feeling she had never felt before. The blood in her veins flowed, and the warmness sent a message. A night of passion can lead to only two things: satisfaction or truth. Truth was that Randy got the message too, and it led to something wonderful. Carmen was ready to receive Randy. She turned over, lying on her back, then Randy gently placed his body on top of hers and put his lips on Carmen's. Passionate as it was, Randy did things to Carmen that he had never done before, and she enjoyed it. Carmen participated and, to her surprise, Randy was in the mood for tricks.

He picked Carmen up, raising her body onto his cord, for which her socket was the perfect fit. He made love to her with feeling, as if no one and nothing else mattered to him. He looked her in the eye as she moved up and down on him. Randy lay back as Carmen rolled back and forth on top of him, planting her flag, claiming what was hers. The speed was fast, but even though Carmen was claiming hers, Randy wanted his. For once he tried something different. He asked Carmen to go to the balcony. She asked why, but his lips to hers stopped her. Randy finally knew what he had, and he was willing to share his love for Carmen with anybody who dared to see. He finished what he started, and by the end all the neighbors knew Randy's name by Carmen's voice yelling, "Yes, Randy, yes!"

Chapter 19

Carmen jumped out of bed, rushed to the bathroom, threw up once again. She cleaned up and was about to climb back into bed when she heard voices from downstairs. She walked in and found that Randy was accompanied by Toni.

"Hey, babe, look who is here," he said. He walked into the kitchen, leaving Toni and Carmen alone.

"What are you doing here, Toni?" said Carmen.

Toni grinned, saying, "Just putting it all on the table."

Toni held a yellow envelope in her hand, one that revealed Carmen and Malcolm's secret. She showed the pictures that she had printed of Carmen and Malcolm together. Carmen was stunned and felt betrayed that Toni would stoop that low. Toni told Carmen to her face that Randy needed to know what a whore his fiancée was, and that if Carmen wasn't going to tell him, she was.

Toni had a thing for Randy, and she thought that if Carmen could get her way, well, why couldn't she? Toni confessed that she had been texting Randy, informing him of the truth, figuring the truth would lead Randy to her arms. Toni smiled as she gave Carmen a wink, saying, "Don't take it personally. You made your bed, now lie in it."

Carmen yelled, "You bitch!" and pushed Toni to the floor. Before Toni could move, Carmen landed on top of her, whupping that ass. Randy rushed from the kitchen and pulled

Carmen off of Toni. Carmen was fired up, but she knew she had to act quickly before Toni told all.

Toni jumped up, screaming "Randy, there's something you should know about Carmen and Malcolm!"

Randy looked at Carmen. She knew she had to come clean and tell Randy the truth. Tears rolled down Carmen's face as she told Randy she had slept with Malcolm and that she might be pregnant. Shock came not only to Toni's eyes but to Randy's as well, as he fell to his knees in tears. Randy faced Carmen, screaming, "What the fuck were you thinking of?" He didn't want to believe it until Toni showed him the pictures and said she sent him all the text messages. Randy was appalled even by Toni's action and said, "Get the hell out of my house!" Randy grabbed Carmen, slamming her to the wall, yelling, "You fucked Malcolm!"

Toni saw Randy's rage and tears and then wanted to step in and take up for Carmen after starting all the mess. Toni screamed, "Stop!" begging Randy to lay off Carmen. Randy then began banging his hands against his head, and without any hesitation he grabbed his keys, saying, "I'm going to kill him!" He took off, speeding recklessly.

Toni told Carmen she was sorry. Carmen screamed, "Get out, get the hell out!" Forgetting all about the wedding rehearsal just hours away, Carmen knew it was over. She fell to her knees crying, asking God for forgiveness, praying that he would make it right.

Chapter 20

Wasting no time, Carmen gathered her thoughts and called Charlotte to cancel the rehearsal. Carmen explained what had happened and that the wedding was over. A seed was planted, but whose was it? Carmen ruined what she had.

Carmen was scared—scared to leave, and surely scared to stay. Word spread that the wedding was off. While driving around looking for trouble, Randy rode by Malcolm's house, catching the dog were he lay. After getting the message about the wedding, Malcolm made no move to even reach out to Randy, yet he reached out to his own needs. Malcolm was in the mood of sexual desire and was getting it on with his next-door neighbor's wife. Randy had no fear but came to do what he had planned and that was to take Malcolm down. He knew Malcolm had a spare key hidden in the lamp that stood outside his front door. Randy politely made himself at home and strolled directly into Malcolm's house, following the moaning and groaning of a woman. Randy kicked the door down, scaring both Malcolm and the woman. She started to scream as she picked up her clothes and ran home, the sheet from Malcolm's bed still wrapped around her.

Malcolm yelled, "What the hell you doing here, Randy?"

"You fucked Carmen!" he yelled back.

Malcolm tried to explain, blaming it all on Carmen, claiming that she came on to him. Randy heard nothing but the phrase "You fucked Carmen" in his head. Man to man, Randy went in for the kill. He whupped that ass, giving every inch of Malcolm's room a new decoration. After all was said and done, Randy walked away like a scorned man, telling Malcolm he was done with him, and so was their partnership.

Randy returned home to find Carmen on her way out with some things in her hands. Carmen stopped, fearing what Randy would do.

"Why did you fuck him?" he asked. He was still furious, but he had gotten the rage out of him on the drive back.

Carmen at first was speechless, afraid of Randy's actions.

"Why did you fuck him?" Randy yelled again.

Still no word from Carmen.

Randy raced up to Carmen, pushing her back against the door, hitting it with his fist until she started screaming, crying, "I'm sorry, I'm sorry! He was there for me when you weren't." Carmen laid it straight as she put it all on the line and told Randy the whole truth. Randy was hurt and beaten up over the whole idea of her and Malcolm, but he concluded he had played a part in why Carmen fell into the arms of another man. For the first time, he listened.

Yes, she had fucked Malcolm Rhodes. Lust gave her what she wanted, her lies cost her Randy's trust, but maybe confessions had just saved her marriage. That would be if Randy doesn't want Revenge.

Eight months later a baby girl was born. A paternity test showed who the father was. In spite of it all, only one potential father showed up for the result. Randy was the father; a life for a life had an impact on Randy. When their child was three, Randy forgave and dropped Carmen's infidelities and let love conquer, to be a father to his daughter. Love overpowered all, and he wedded his bride.

Lust, lies, and confessions transformed into: loving again, living through faith, and comforting open wounds.

From the author: Marriage is a huge step. Without God first, as the head of your life and household, to pull both loose ends together to bond as one, your dedication to one another, respect and love can lead to destruction. Let God be your salvation, and love one another.

LaShae Berry

www.ingramcontent.com/pod-product-compliance
Ingram Content Group UK Ltd.
Pitfield, Milton Keynes, MK11 3LW, UK
UKHW041845190726
13854UKWH00002B/719

9 781480 810815